A modern approach

Reading and writing should flow through the natural activities and interests of the child. The next most important aid is a series of books designed to stimulate and interest him and to give daily practice at the right level.

Educational experts from five Caribbean countries have co-operated with the author to design and produce this Ladybird Sunstart Reading Scheme. Their work has been influenced by (a) the widely accepted piece of research 'Key Words to Literacy[1]' adapted here for tropical countries. This word list has been used to accelerate learning in the early stages. (b) The work of Dr. Dennis Craig[2] of the School of Education, U.W.I., and other specialists who have carried out research in areas where the English language is being taught to young children whose natural speech on entering school is a patois or dialect varying considerably from standard English.

[1] Key Words to Literacy *by J McNally and W Murray, published by The Teacher Publishing Co Ltd, Derbyshire House, Kettering, Northants, England.*

[2] An experiment in teaching English *by Dennis R Craig, Caribbean Universities Press, also* Torch *(Vol. 22, No. 2), Journal of the Ministry of Education, Jamaica.*

THE LADYBIRD SUNSTART READING SCHEME consists of six books and three workbooks. These are graded and written with a controlled vocabulary and plentiful repetition. They are fully illustrated.

Book 1 'Lucky dip' (for beginners) is followed by Book 2 'On the beach'. Workbook A is parallel to these and covers the vocabulary of both books. The workbook reinforces the words learned in the readers, teaches handwriting and introduces phonic training.

Book 3 'The kite' and Book 4 'Animals, birds and fish' follow Books 1 and 2, and are supported by Workbook B. This reinforces the vocabulary of Books 3 and 4 and again contains handwriting exercises and phonic training.

Book 5 'I wish' and Book 6 'Guess what?' with Workbook C complete the scheme.

The illustrated handbook (free) for parents and teachers is entitled 'A Guide to the Teaching of Reading'.

For classroom use there are two boxes of large flash cards which cover the first three books.

BOOK 4
The Ladybird SUNSTART Reading Scheme
(a 'Key Words' Reading Scheme)

Animals, birds and fish

by W. MURRAY

with illustrations by MARTIN AITCHISON

Ladybird Books Loughborough
in collaboration with Longman Caribbean Ltd

On the water

Joy and Ken are with Mother and Father. They have come here to see the fish, animals and birds that live by the water. A man Father knows is with them.

They all get in a boat. Joy and Ken look happy. They want to go on the water.

"Do you know the way we go?" Ken asks.

"Yes," says Father. "We know the way. This is not the first time that we have come here."

They want to see all they can, so the boat does not go fast. Ken looks into the water and Joy looks up at the trees.

"I like it here," says Joy. "We must come again."

The boat goes by a flamingo in the water.

a flamingo

The flamingo is a beautiful bird with long legs and a long neck. The colour of this flamingo is pink.

"Are all flamingoes pink?" Ken asks Father.

"No, not all of them are pink," says Father. "There are some red ones here."

"Can they fly?" asks Ken.

"Yes, flamingoes can fly," says Father.

"Look up," says Mother. "Look up there. You can see some flying up there."

Ken says, "What long legs a flamingo has!"

"Yes, and what a long neck it has!" says Joy.

"Here are some others," says Mother, as the boat goes on. "I like the colours. They are all beautiful birds."

Some of the flamingoes they see are red and some are pink.

There is mud by the water. Ken says that he can see something on the mud.

"Yes, I can see it," says Father. "It is an alligator."

"I do not like the look of it," says Joy.

"No, it looks dangerous," says Mother.

"It is as big as a man," Ken says.

As the boat goes by, they see other alligators. Some are very big. One is in the water. The others lie in the sun, on the mud.

"What do they eat?" asks Joy.

"Alligators eat fish and little animals that live by the water, or in the water," says Father.

Mother says, "Alligators like to lie on the mud, in the sun, for a long time."

an alligator

They go on for a long way, and then the boat stops. They stop so that they all can eat.

There are no alligators here, but they do not get out of the boat. There is mud, but no sand.

Mother has a box and a bag. She gets out something for everyone to eat. They sit in the boat and eat.

As Ken and Joy eat oranges they look into the water at the fish. The man sits with the children and tells them the names of some of the kinds of fish.

Then the children see a bird in a tree. They know that the bird is a scarlet ibis.

a scarlet ibis

The scarlet ibis is a beautiful bird. Its neck and its legs are long, but not as long as the neck and legs of the flamingo. It is red, not pink, with some black on its wings.

The scarlet ibis likes to live by water, as the flamingo does. It feeds in the water.

"I like its scarlet colour," says Joy. "I want a scarlet dress."

Ken says, "I can see a little black on the wings of the birds as they fly."

As the sun goes down they see more scarlet ibis. Then more and more of them fly by.

"This is what we have come to see," says Mother. "They are very beautiful."

wings

The sun goes down and it gets dark. It is not very dark, but time to go back.

Then a bat flies by. A bat has wings and looks something like a bird, but it is not a bird. It is a little animal that flies. It can fly in the dark.

More bats come. Then more and more. The children do not like bats.

Father tells them that these bats will not hurt them. "They will not come into the boat," he says. "These bats do not hurt people."

As the boat goes back, Mother sings to the children. They like her to sing. Then she tells them to sing and they sing with her.

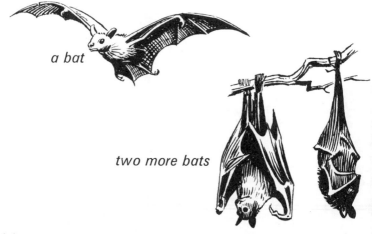

a bat

two more bats

The Aquarium

One day, this mother asks her two children, Dave and Sandra, "Do you want to go to the Aquarium?"

"Yes please, I do," says Sandra.

Dave says, "Yes, I want to go. I know something about the Aquarium, but I have not been there."

"Have you been to this Aquarium?" Sandra asks her mother.

"Yes," her mother says. "I have been to this one and to some others." She tells them what they will see.

Then they go to the Aquarium.

First they see the turtles. Some of these are under the water. The man there gets a turtle out of the water for the children to see. The turtle is not hurt and it does not hurt the man.

He tells them that this turtle lives in the water.

a turtle

Some turtles live in the water all the time. Other turtles can live on land or in water.

The back or shell of the turtle is very hard. This hard shell is something like a house for the turtle. It can pull in its neck, its head and its legs under the shell. Then it cannot be hurt.

This hard shell helps the turtle to live a long time. A turtle can live to be very old.

Tortoises are very like turtles, but tortoises live on the land all the time. Some tortoises are very big.

Mother says that she knows of one tortoise so big that a girl or boy can get on its back. This does not hurt the tortoise as it is so big. Children must not hurt animals.

a tortoise

At the Aquarium, the children see fish of many kinds and many colours. Some of the colours are beautiful. The children can read the names of some kinds of fish. Mother reads some of the other names to them.

Dave sees a man in the water. "Look, Sandra," he says, "that man is in the water with the fish."

"What is he going to do?" asks Sandra.

"He is going to feed the fish," says Dave. "You will see."

The man under the water feeds the fish. Many of the fish come to him. They know him.

Some other people come to see the man under the water feed the fish.

ANGEL FISH
COLLUVISH

"We must see the dolphins," says Dave.

"Yes," Sandra says. "I have read about dolphins at school. I read that the dolphin lives in the sea, but it is not a fish. It must come up for air to live."

"I know," says Dave. "I know that it must have air. Come on, here are the dolphins!"

One of the dolphins plays with a ball. One does a kind of a dance on the water. Some others jump out of the water into the air.

A man who works at the Aquarium comes to feed fish to the dolphins. They jump into the air for the fish.

Mother tells the children more about the dolphins, and how they can help men who work at sea under water.

a dolphin

The Zoo

Another day, Father and Mother take the two children to the Zoo. They know that children like going to the Zoo to see the many kinds of animals there.

"Let's see the monkeys first," says Dave.

They go to where the monkeys live. Some of the monkeys sit in the sun. Others jump from tree to tree.

One monkey takes a girl's hat. He runs away from another monkey who tries to take it from him.

"I like the little ones," says Sandra. "Look at that one !"

A boy has a balloon on a string. A little black and white monkey wants to pull it away from him.

a monkey

Sandra likes cats. She wants to have a cat in her house. She wants to look after it and play with it.

Does this animal look like a cat? It is not like the one that Sandra wants. It is a cat, another kind of cat.

This is a lion, a big, strong lion. This very strong lion is in a Zoo.

a cat

a lion

People like to look at the lion and to see it lie in the sun. But they cannot play with it, or have it in the house. It is dangerous, very dangerous.

A lion can kill you. It can kill and eat other big animals.

Here is another kind of cat. It is a tiger. A tiger is big and strong. It can be as strong as a lion.

A lion likes to lie in the sun, but the tiger does not. It likes to be away from the sun, by some trees, or in grass where there is some water. This tiger lies in some grass.

The tiger has stripes on its head, neck, back and legs. The stripes are black. These black stripes help it to hide in the grass or trees.

The tiger can hide in a tree, and jump down on to the back of another animal to kill and eat it. It is dangerous to man.

a tiger

some grass

Dave and Sandra go to see the parrots at the Zoo. They know a girl at school who has a parrot for a pet. It can talk a little.

They learn that there are many kinds of parrot. There are big ones, little ones and parrots of all colours. Some parrots fly and others cannot fly.

"Can all parrots learn to talk?" Dave asks the man with the parrots.

"No," he says. "Not many kinds of parrot can learn to talk. The kinds that do talk take a long time to learn." He tells them that children who have pets must learn how to look after them.

On the way home the children talk about the pets they want to have.

a parrot

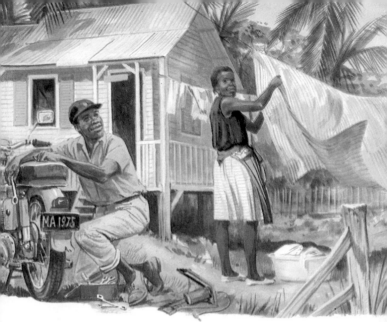

A walk

Barry and Gail want to go for a walk to see what they can find. First they ask their mother if they can go.

"Yes," she says. "You can go for a walk, but take the dog. Don't go where it is dangerous and don't get in the mud."

The dog is a pet, but he is a big, strong dog.

"Come on," says Barry to the dog. "We are going for a walk." The dog jumps up. He wants to go for a walk.

The sun is out. They walk in the grass by some trees. The dog runs off but they know that he will come back to them again.

Gail wants to look for a humming bird.

a humming bird

Barry cannot see Gail. "Where are you?" he calls to her. He calls again, "Don't hide, Gail. Where are you?"

Gail calls out, "Over here by the flowers. Come over here."

Barry runs to where Gail is.

She can hear a humming sound. She knows that it is the sound of a humming bird.

"Can you hear that sound?" Gail asks Barry. "Can you hear the humming bird?"

"Yes," says Barry. "Where is it?"

They look for the humming bird by the flowers. They know that the very little bird makes a humming sound with its wings.

"There it is," says Barry. "Look over there by that flower."

"What a beautiful little bird it is!" says Gail.

some flowers

As they walk, Barry and Gail see men at work on the land. They know some of the men and stop and talk to them.

They look at animals and birds and trees and flowers. They see many butterflies.

"Some butterflies are going up and down in the air as they fly," says Gail. "They look as if they dance as they fly."

"Butterflies come from caterpillars," says Barry. "There are all kinds of caterpillars and butterflies. They don't live long."

Gail says, "Caterpillars come from little eggs and the eggs come from the butterflies. Mother says it makes her happy to see the colours of butterflies in the sun."

eggs   *caterpillar*   *butterfly* 37

The children know the names of some of the other birds. They see a little yellow and brown bird fly by. It flies fast, but not as fast as a humming bird.

"I know what that is," says Gail. "It is a keskidee. I can tell by its yellow and brown colours."

"Yes, and the keskidee has white on its head. The white looks something like a hat," says Barry.

Then they hear the bird call. The call sounds like "Keskidee, Keskidee."

"Its call is like its name," says Barry. "That is why they call it a keskidee."

"Look," says Gail. "You can see it catch flies. It has to fly quickly to do that."

a keskidee

The children walk on. Then Gail sees something small move in the grass. "Is that a snake?" she asks.

"No," says Barry, going over to look. "It is like a snake, but it has legs. It is a lizard."

They know something about lizards. They know that there are very many kinds. Some are big, others very big, but most are small. Some lizards live in trees. Most lizards are not dangerous.

All lizards can move quickly, so quickly that they can catch insects. Most people do not like lizards, but some do. Barry knows a man who lets one small lizard into the house to catch insects.

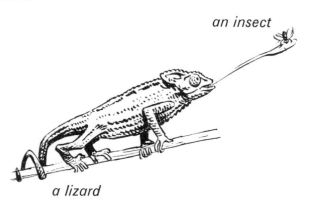

an insect

a lizard

Barry and Gail go on to the beach. They like to walk on the sand by the water.

"Do you know that turtles lay their eggs in the sand?" asks Gail.

"Yes," says Barry. "I know that turtles come out of the sea, lay their eggs in the sand and then go back into the water. They don't look after their eggs."

The children come to where some men are fishing. They see them catch some fish.

"I want to go fishing in a boat," says Barry. "I am going to ask Dad if he will take me fishing with him."

"Yes, and I am going to come with you," says Gail.

a boy fishing

Fishing at sea

"I am going fishing," says Father to Mother. "I will take Barry and Gail with me. They want to come. Do you want to come?"

"No, thank you," says Mother. "I will come another time."

Father and another man get into a boat with the children and they all go out to sea.

They see a flying fish jump out of the water. It goes through the air by their boat. The flying fish does not fly like a bird. It has no wings, but its large fins look like wings. These large fins help it to move quickly through the air. Flying fish can be caught with nets.

The two men in this boat have no nets with them. They want to catch some very large fish, not flying fish.

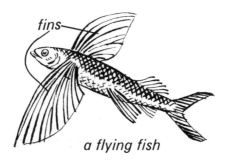

fins

a flying fish

They see the large fish that the men want to catch. The children keep out of the way of the men as they fish. They don't want to get hurt.

It takes a long time to catch some of the large fish. They are strong and can move very quickly through the water. But the boat is fast and the men know what to do. They have caught many fish before.

Father pulls a very big fish up to the boat. Before he can pull it in, it fights back and gets away.

Then the other man catches one. Father helps him get it into the boat. After this, two more fish are caught, but not before the boat goes a long way.

At home

Barry and Gail are at home. They like to read at home. They read how a mongoose kills a snake.

The snake is big and very dangerous. It fights the mongoose. The mongoose is a small animal, but it is very strong.

In the fight the mongoose moves fast. If it does not move very quickly the snake will kill it.

The fight goes on for a long time before the mongoose kills the snake.

Barry and Gail read more about animals, birds and fish. Gail likes to read about beautiful butterflies, humming birds and fish most of all. Barry wants to learn more about large animals like the lion and the tiger.

a mongoose

49

Can you read the words when you cover the pictures?

1 Flamingoes feed in the water.

2 This alligator lies on the mud in the sun.

3 The hard shell of this turtle is a dark colour.

4 The boy sits on the back of a large tortoise.

5 Dolphins can jump out of the water.

6 Monkeys like to live where there are trees.

7 The girl has a cat at home for a pet.

8 The lion is very strong and dangerous.

9 The dark stripes of a tiger help it to hide.

10 Most parrots cannot learn to talk.

11 These men work on the land.

12 A beautiful butterfly flies over the flowers.

13 The keskidee is brown, yellow and white.

14 She sees a snake in the grass.

15 The lizard catches and eats insects.

16 A turtle lays its eggs in the sand.

17 They go for a walk with their dog.

18 "I am going fishing," says the boy.

19 The large fins of the flying fish help it to move quickly through the air.

20 A mongoose can fight and kill a snake.

Words new to the series used in this book

Total number of words 101